For Dad. B.M.

With big thanks to Catherine and little Sam. E.B.

First published in Great Britain in 2012 by Andersen Press Ltd., 20 Vauxhall Bridge Road, London SWIV 2SA.
Published in Australia by Random House Australia Pty., Level 3, 100 Pacific Highway, North Sydney, NSW 2060.
Text copyright © Brett McKee, 2012. Illustration copyright © Ella Burfoot, 2012.
The rights of Brett McKee and Ella Burfoot to be identified as the author and illustrator of this work
have been asserted by them in accordance with the Copyright, Designs and Patents Act, 1988.
All rights reserved. Colour separated in Switzerland by Photolitho AG, Zürich.
Printed and bound in Singapore by Tien Wah Press.
Ella Burfoot has used watercolour and coloured pencils in this book.

10   9   8   7   6   5   4   3   2   1

British Library Cataloguing in Publication Data available.
ISBN 978 1 84939 291 4 (Hardback)
ISBN 978 1 84939 313 3 (Paperback)
This book has been printed on acid-free paper

Monsters Don't Cry!

Brett McKee Ella Burfoot

ANDERSEN PRESS

Archie awoke with a shout in the night.
Only a dream, but what a terrible fright.

Monsters may roar,
may growl or just sigh,
But monsters are strong,
monsters don't cry!

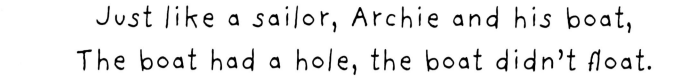

Just like a sailor, Archie and his boat,
The boat had a hole, the boat didn't float.

Monsters may roar,
may growl or just sigh,
But monsters are strong,
monsters don't cry!

Archie, brave Archie, to his alarm,
Was chased by a goat,
all over the farm.

Monsters may roar,
may growl or just sigh,
But monsters are strong,
monsters don't cry!

While swinging his swing, Archie swung too high,
Archie let go but monsters don't fly.

Monsters may roar, may growl or just sigh,
But monsters are strong, monsters don't cry!

Courageously Archie climbed up a tree . . .

Then he got stuck and so missed his tea.

Monsters may roar,
may growl or just sigh,
But monsters are strong,
monsters don't cry!

Run racing with Daddy, there in the wood,
A branch hit Archie, it didn't feel good.

Monsters may roar, may growl or just sigh,
But monsters are strong, monsters don't cry!

Cake, Archie loved, it tasted so yummy,
He ate and ate and upset his tummy.
Monsters may roar, may growl or just sigh,
But monsters are strong, monsters don't cry!

Archie, young Archie entered a maze,
He soon got lost and had to be saved.

Monsters may roar, may growl or just sigh,
But monsters are strong, monsters don't cry!

Riding his bike,
Archie went round
and round,

Until he made himself
dizzy . . .

and fell on the ground.

Monsters may roar, may growl or just sigh,
But monsters are strong, monsters don't cry!

Mummy and Daddy and Archie all three,
Ended their picnic because of a bee.
Monsters may roar, may growl or just sigh,
But monsters are strong, monsters don't cry!

Archie as usual took
Teddy to bed,
He gave him a hug . . .

and off came his head.

Monsters they roar, they growl or just sigh,
And sometimes even a monster will cry!

Archie, brave Archie was feeling much better,
Now that Teddy had been put back together.
Monsters may roar, may growl or just sigh,
But monsters need love if ever they cry!